JULIE
SYKES

ILLUSTRATED BY
NATHAN REED

PARROT
PANDEMONIUM

KINGFISHER
NEW YORK

For Sarah, Diane, and Jill—J. S.
For Ella Rose—N. R.

KINGFISHER
LONDON & NEW YORK

Text copyright © 2009 by Julie Sykes
Illustrations copyright © 2009 by Nathan Reed
Published in the United States by Kingfisher,
175 Fifth Ave., New York, NY 10010
Kingfisher is an imprint of Macmillan Children's Books, London.
All rights reserved.

Distributed in the U.S. by Macmillan, 175 Fifth Ave., New York, NY 10010
Distributed in Canada by H.B. Fenn and Company Ltd., 34 Nixon Road,
Bolton, Ontario L7E 1W2

Library of Congress Cataloging-in-Publication data has been applied for.

ISBN: 978-0-7534-6219-5

Kingfisher books are available for special promotions and premiums. For details contact:
Special Markets Department, Macmillan, 175 Fifth Avenue, New York, NY 10010.

For more information, please visit www.kingfisherpublications.com

First American Edition September 2009
Printed and bound in the U.K. by CPI Mackays, Chatham ME5 8TD
1 3 5 7 9 8 6 4 2

CONTENTS

CHAPTER ONE
ANOTHER JOB

Max was on his way out to the yard when the telephone rang.

"I'll get it," he said.

"It'll be for you anyway," said Mom. "It always is."

Max snatched up the phone and was almost deafened by the person on the other end.

"Is that Max Barker?"

"Yes," said Max, hoping this was another job. Max was a pet sitter. He loved animals, but he couldn't have any of his own because his big sister, Alice, was allergic to them.

"Hi, Max. My name's Captain Boom. I need a pet sitter to look after Squawk, my parrot. I'm going away tomorrow for two days, so could you come and meet him now?"

"Sure," said Max, sticking out his tongue at Alice as she shoved past him. "Where do you live?"

"At Blue Water Marina, on a boat called

the *Leaky Dip*. You can't miss it. It's the oldest thing here besides me." Captain Boom laughed. "How long will it take you to get here?"

"Ten minutes," said Max.

"See you in ten minutes then," said Captain Boom, hanging up.

Max quickly wrote Captain Boom's details in his pet-sitter notebook and then pulled on his sneakers.

"Going somewhere?" asked Mom.

"Yes," said Max. "To Blue Water Marina to meet Captain Boom. He wants me to look after his parrot."

"But you don't know anything about parrots," said Mom.

"I do," Max replied. "Alice is like a parrot. She squawks a lot and she's always repeating herself."

"Moooom! Tell him off!" squawked Alice.

Max grinned. "See what I mean! Bye, Mom. Bye, Alice."

"Be back by five," called Mrs. Barker.

As Max rode to the marina, he tried to imagine what Captain Boom would be like. He had a very loud voice for an old person. Would Squawk be old, too? Max imagined an elderly bird with faded eyes and hardly any feathers.

"Pretty Polly," Max chirped, imitating the parrot in the local pet store.

It didn't take long for Max to find the *Leaky Dip*. Captain Boom had been right; his boat was definitely the oldest one at the marina. Chaining his bike to a mooring, Max eyed the *Leaky Dip*'s gangplank. It was falling to pieces and didn't look very safe. Carefully, he stepped onto it.

The gangplank creaked, and Max waited a moment before taking another step forward. He was just taking a third step when someone bellowed, "STOP!"

The voice was so fierce that Max froze immediately.

"Put your hands in the air."

Max raised his arms. The rickety gangplank wobbled, and he stared ahead, fixing his gaze on the *Leaky Dip*'s main mast to stop himself from losing his balance and falling into the water.

"Walk forward, nice and slow. That's it. Now, lie face-down on the deck."

"What?" exclaimed Max. "No way! I . . ."

"Do it!" roared the voice. "Or I'll blow you to the other side of the world with a cannonball."

CHAPTER TWO
ONBOARD THE LEAKY DIP

Max did as he was told, feeling his pet-sitter notebook slide out of his pocket as he lay down. He wanted to pick it up, but he didn't dare. Being blown to the other side of the world wasn't on his agenda. Not today.

"Who are you?" snarled the voice. "Why were you sneaking up my gangplank?"

"I'm Max Barker. I'm the pet sitter," said Max, as clearly as he could with his mouth squashed against the deck's dusty surface.

"Of course you are!" said a deeper and much more friendly voice. "Shiver me shoes, are you all right? I've been meaning to fix that gangplank for ages. Did you trip over the loose part?"

Two strong hands hauled Max to his feet, and he found himself staring up at a huge man with bright blue eyes, a curly black beard, and one hoop earring. Captain Boom must have been joking on the phone. He wasn't old at all and looked just like a pirate. He was dressed in a white shirt, gold-buttoned vest, and raggedy three-quarter-length pants.

"Captain Billy Boom," he said,

shaking Max's hand. "Thanks for coming so quickly, and I'm really sorry about that gangplank. I'll fix it before I go, and that's a promise."

"Er, great," said Max, staring around to see whom the other voice belonged to.

But besides Captain Boom, the deck was empty.

"Weird!" muttered Max, sure he hadn't imagined the other voice.

He rescued his notebook and flicked through it until he found the right page.

"Captain Boom, the *Leaky Dip*, Blue Water Marina. Your parrot's named Squawk and you're going away for two days."

"That's right." Captain Boom sighed. "It's Treasure trouble."

"Too bad," said Max sympathetically.

"Did you forget where
you buried it?"

Captain Boom
roared with laughter.

"Not treasure," he
spluttered. "Wish it was,
though. No, I'm going to
visit Treasure. She's my sister,
and believe me when I say she's trouble!"

"So is my big sister, Alice," said Max. "Is
Treasure your big sister, too?"

"You could say that. She's big anyway,"
Captain Boom said, chuckling. "But enough
about Treasure. Come meet Squawk."

Captain Boom led the way across the
deck, behind the mast, and up five steps to
the quarterdeck. Max followed, weaving his
way around piles of frayed ropes, tattered
sails, and one very rusty cannon.

"'Scuse the mess,"
said Captain Boom.
"It never used to be like
this. The clutter built
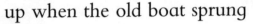
up when the old boat sprung
so many leaks that I had
to stop sailing her. I'll
clean up before I
go, and that's a
promise."

Captain Boom stopped at
a wooden mast a little bit smaller than
the *Leaky Dip*'s main one and bellowed,
"Squawk, Max is here. Come down and
say hello."

Max squinted upward and quickly
realized something.

"That's not a mast—it's a tree!"

The tree looked like it had come straight

from a tropical rainforest. Max ran his hand across its bark expecting it to be fake, but the tree was real.

"Squawk," shouted Captain Boom, "come meet Max!"

Shielding his eyes from the sun, Max stared between the tree's feathery leaves, hoping to catch a glimpse of Squawk. Nothing. The parrot stayed hidden.

"That's so cool!" said Max. "A real tree growing on a boat. I bet Squawk loves it."

"That's right," said Captain Boom.

"I got it when I got Squawk. Parrots and trees go together like sea and sand, maps and treasure, sharks and . . . SQUAWK! Get down from there right now. Don't think I can't see you!"

There was an angry screech from behind Max. He wheeled around in time to see a red blur hurtling toward him from the rigging of the main mast.

"Duck!" roared Captain Boom.

"It's not. It's definitely a parrot," shouted Max, covering his head with his hands as the feathered cannonball hurtled closer.

CHAPTER THREE

SQUAWK SPEAKS

"**S**quawk, STOP!" roared Captain Boom. "That's NOT funny. Behave yourself or I'll throw you in the bilge!"

The bird stopped middive, skidding to a halt about three feet above the captain's head. Then, flying very slowly, he landed on Captain Boom's shoulder.

"Nice emergency landing," said Max, impressed.

"Max, meet Squawk." Captain Boom lightly stroked his parrot's beak. "And, Squawk, meet Max, your pet sitter."

"Hello, Squawk," said Max.

Squawk fluffed up
his magnificent red, blue,
and yellow feathers and
then stuck his beak in the air.

"Squawk," said Captain Boom
with a note of warning, "say hello to Max."

Reluctantly, Squawk fixed Max with his
small black eyes.

"M . . . A . . . T," he said slowly.
"M-A-T. Hello, Mat."

"Max," said Max and Captain Boom
together.

"Mat," repeated Squawk stubbornly.

"It's Max!" yelled Captain Boom.

"Mat," said Squawk, giving Max a
hard stare. "Mat. Cat. Cat, mat. The cat
sat on Mat."

Max laughed.

"Very good." He chuckled. "A talking

parrot with a sense of humor."

"Squawk's got a sense of humor all right," said Captain Boom dryly. "And as for talking, he could talk the mainsail right off its mast. Ouch! Don't bite my ear. And while we're on the don'ts . . ." Captain Boom paused to make sure both Squawk and Max were listening. "Don't let Squawk go anywhere near the mast. He loves it up there, but he's banned because he's a menace. He fiddles with the rigging, and that causes accidents. And please DON'T upset my neighbor, Captain Becky Bones."

Captain Boom pointed to a fancy boat moored a short distance from the *Leaky Dip*. A skull and crossbones flew from each of its three masts, but not the usual type of skull and crossbones. Each of the skulls on Captain Becky Bones's flags had red blood oozing from its eye sockets. Max shivered and wished that Becky's boat was moored somewhere a bit farther away, like Australia.

"Becky Bones, captain of the *Shark's Teeth* and terror of the seas," whispered Captain Boom. "Upset her at your peril!"

Squawk crossed his eyes and made a gagging sound as if someone were strangling him.

Captain Boom grinned.

"And she'd have you for parrot pie, too," he said cheerfully. "Okay, Max, let's step below and I'll show you what Squawk likes to eat."

Leaving Squawk in his tree, Captain Boom climbed down a creaky ladder from the main deck. The space downstairs was even messier than up above. Gingerly, Max followed the captain through a large cabin with a squishy sofa and small television and on into a tiny kitchen.

"This is the galley," Captain Boom proudly announced.

Max squeezed in after him, nose wrinkled, expecting the worst, but the galley was spotlessly clean and tidy. Cooking utensils dangled from hooks on the wall, silver pans hung over a tiny stove, and strings of garlic and onions hung around the porthole.

"I love cooking," explained Captain Boom, patting his enormous stomach. "And Squawk and I both love eating."

He pulled open a cabinet door, and Max stared in amazement. The shelves were full of plastic containers, all neatly labeled in black pen.

"Walnuts, Brazil nuts, pecans, cashews," read Max. "Wheat, corn, sunflower, oats, linseed."

"Squawk likes variety," said Captain Boom, pulling open another door to reveal a fridge stashed with oranges, apples, grapes, cherries, mangoes, kiwifruit, carrots, beans, and much more. "I'll write you a menu for each day. Make sure he has plenty of fresh water, and at bedtime he gets a treat of toast covered in honey then cut into small pieces and dipped in tea."

"Not much, then!" joked Max. "Maybe I'll move in here. All I get at bedtime is a lecture on brushing my teeth."

"Feel free," said Captain Boom. "I'll make up a bunk for you in the spare cabin before I go."

Max laughed.

"Thanks, but I was just kidding. Mom and Dad complain I'm never home as it is."

"Well, the offer stands, if you change your mind," said Captain Boom. He reached up, took a battered canister from a cabinet on the wall, and shook out its contents. Max gaped at the tangle of jewelery, coins, and bills that spilled over the countertop.

"How do you want to be paid? Jewelry or cash?" asked Captain Boom.

"Cash, please," said Max quickly. "I'm saving up for a new bike, and the store takes only cash."

"Not very adventurous of it," said Captain Boom.

"Tell me about it." Max sighed. "It does exchanges, but the man wouldn't even consider swapping my sister for the bike I want."

Captain Boom laughed.

"I tried swapping Treasure once for Becky's third-best cannon. When Becky discovered Treasure was my sister, she tied me to the mast and used me as a target to practice her knife-throwing trick." Captain Boom shuddered. "You don't mess with Captain Becky Bones!"

As Max left the *Leaky Dip*, Becky Bones was sitting on her deck peeling an orange with a sword. Seeing Max watching her, she suddenly threw the orange up into the air. The sword flashed, and then orange segments rained from the sky. Deftly, Becky caught the pieces on the sword's blade and popped each one into her mouth.

"Whew," said Max, hopping onto his bike and pedaling out of the marina. "I'd rather arm wrestle an octopus than upset her!"

CHAPTER FOUR
A CRY FOR HELP

Max couldn't wait to start his new pet-sitting job. The following morning, before breakfast, he went on the Internet to look for information on parrots.

"Parrots are noisy, sociable birds. They are quick to learn and are good mimics," Max read. "Pet parrots need challenging toys to keep them from getting bored. Climbing is a favorite pastime. They shouldn't be left alone with furniture or electrical wires, as they might damage them."

There were lots of pictures of parrot toys, some of which reminded Max of the toys he'd had as a baby. Mom had kept all his favorite ones and, going through the closet under the stairs, Max found his old wooden shape sorter.

"Squawk will love this," he said, wiping off the dust.

"What've you got there?" asked Alice, sneaking up behind him. "Ooooh, do you need help, little Max? Can't you figure out which shape goes through which hole?"

"There's only one hole big enough to fit these shapes through and that's your mouth," said Max. "Open wide, sis!"

"Hmph," snorted Alice. "You're the one

with the big mouth. Watch what you say, Max, 'cause one day that mouth is going to get you into BIG trouble!"

"You wish!" said Max, slipping past Alice and putting the shape sorter in a plastic bag, ready to take with him when he left to visit Squawk.

It was still early when Max arrived at the marina. No one was around as he chained his bike to a mooring. With the plastic bag in one hand, Max stepped onto the *Leaky Dip*'s gangplank. If anything, the gangplank was even more wobbly than it had been the day before.

"Captain Boom kept his promise to fix it . . . not!" muttered Max.

"STOP!"

It was the same fierce voice that Max

had heard the day before, and once again he froze.

"Put your hands in the air."

"What? No way. Look, I . . ."

BANG . . . WHOOOO . . . SPLASH!

Max never saw the cannonball, but it sounded very close, and he immediately raised his hands above his head.

"That was just a warning," said the scary voice. "The next ball's got your name on it. So let's try again. Hands in the air and walk forward nice and slow."

As slow as a sloth, Max inched his way along the gangplank until the voice called out again, "Good. Now hop."

"But—" squeaked Max.

"HOP!" roared the voice.

Max hopped, and his heart hopped, too, each time his foot left the rickety gangplank. Would he make it or would he end up falling into the water? Six

agonizing hops later and Max was safely aboard the *Leaky Dip*. He risked a quick look around, but the deck was empty.

"STAND STILL!" roared the voice suddenly. "What's in the bag?"

"A toy," said Max, pulling out the shape sorter. "It's for Squawk to play with. Squawk's a parrot. I'm—"

"I know who Squawk is! Squawk doesn't like toys for babies and neither do I. Next time bring candy."

"Candy?" repeated Max in surprise.

"Gummi bears," said the voice. "So I can pull their heads off. Bring me gummi bears tomorrow or I'll pull your head off instead. Got that? Good. Now hop to it."

Max stared around, but he could see no sign of the speaker. Was it safe to stay on the boat or should he leave?

I've got to stay, Max decided. *I can't leave Squawk here on his own.*

Nervously, Max crossed the main deck to the small aviary that Captain Boom had shown him the day before. Although Squawk was uncaged by day, Captain Boom insisted on locking him up at night.

"People steal parrots," he'd told Max. "They're worth a lot of money."

Squawk was still asleep. Head tucked under one multicolored wing, he was snoring loudly.

Max chuckled. He'd never heard of a snoring parrot.

"Squawk," he called softly, "wake up. It's Max. Your pet sitter."

Squawk woke up so quickly that Max suspected he hadn't been asleep at all. He wondered if Squawk had heard the strange voice and seen Max hopping up the gangplank. It was an embarrassing thought.

"Time for breakfast," said Max, unlocking the aviary. "It's mangoes this morning."

"Hello, Mat," said Squawk. "Hello, doormat."

Max was thinking up a smart reply when a childlike cry made him spin around.

"Help!"

It sounded like a little girl, and it was coming from the top of the mast.

"Help!"

Screwing up his eyes against the morning sun, Max scanned the mast, but he couldn't see anyone there.

"Where are you?" he called.

"Up here."

"Where? I can't see you."

"I'm in the crow's-nest."

Max stared up to the special lookout post at the top of the mast. It was empty. The little girl must have been very tiny if he couldn't see her over the top of its sides.

"Who are you? What are you doing up there?" shouted Max.

"I got lost. I thought if I climbed up high, I might be able to see where I was going."

"Come down," said Max. "Come down slowly, and I'll help you find your way home."

"I can't!" The voice rose to a squeal. "I'm stuck! I'm too scared to move!"

"Ooooh!" Squawk stepped out of the aviary and waddled toward Max. "Sounds like a job for me. I'll fly up and help her down, shall I?"

"Ha! So you *can* talk properly!" exclaimed Max. "I knew it!"

Max was used to pet sitting for talking animals, and Captain Boom had said that Squawk was a chatterbox.

"Course I can talk, bilge bucket! You humans! You're all the same. You think

33

you're the only ones born with a tongue!"

"Help!" called the little girl. "I'm going to fall."

"Quick! I'll go." Squawk flapped his feathers as he prepared to take off.

"No!" said Max. "You're not allowed up the mast. I'll go."

"Spoilsport," said Squawk. "Well, don't go shouting for help when you get stuck, too!"

"I won't," said Max. "I'm good at climbing."

The mast was higher than it looked. Max climbed as fast as he dared while calling comforting words to the little girl, who was now crying. Reaching the crow's-nest, Max sighed with relief. He'd made it! He raised his head over the top of the platform, kicked his legs, and arrived in a heap. Quickly sitting up, Max stared around in surprise. The

crow's-nest was
empty.

"Hello?" shouted
Max. "Where are you?"

"Down here."
The little girl dissolved
into giggles.

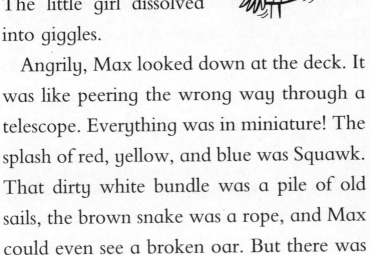

Angrily, Max looked down at the deck. It
was like peering the wrong way through a
telescope. Everything was in miniature! The
splash of red, yellow, and blue was Squawk.
That dirty white bundle was a pile of old
sails, the brown snake was a rope, and Max
could even see a broken oar. But there was
no sign of the little girl!

"Where down there?" shouted Max,
somewhat irritated.

"Here . . . And here . . . And here . . .
Over here . . . I'm here!"

The little girl's voice seemed to come at Max from all directions. It echoed from down on the deck right up to the Jolly Roger at the very top of the mast. For a second, Max wondered if he was losing his mind, and then suddenly he got it! He'd been had! The voices and noises weren't real. None of them. Not the cannon fire, nor the scary voice that had forced him to hop up the gangplank. It was all a trick. And if he wasn't mistaken, Squawk was to blame.

"Parrots are good mimics," Max remembered. "And very good at throwing their voices, too, by the sound of it!" he muttered.

Max started to laugh. "Blazing beaks!" he exclaimed. "I've been tricked by a parrot!"

CHAPTER FIVE
UPSETTING BECKY BONES

Max then heard Squawk's raucous cries of laughter. The parrot probably thought he was a real dunce, falling for his tricks so easily!

Max gazed around, determined to make the most of the view before he climbed back down to the deck. He could see why Squawk liked playing on the mast. It was wonderful being so high up. It was also a great place for spying. Max could clearly see the *Leaky Dip*'s neighbor, the *Shark's Teeth*, and even in miniature she was a boat to admire.

"I'd love a ride on her," said Max wistfully. "I bet she's really fast."

Max loved fast things. Unfortunately his parents didn't. Mom was the worst. She drove so slowly that even tractors passed her! Onboard the *Shark's Teeth*, a door burst open and Captain Becky Bones came running up on deck.

"Ahoy there, *Leaky Dip*," she bellowed. "Cut the noise. I'm trying to listen to the shipping news!"

Max chuckled softly as Squawk immediately stopped laughing. Then, to his horror, his own voice shouted back at Becky, "Ahoy there, *Shark's Teeth*. Get a life. Listen to the music channel instead!"

Max whipped around, almost expecting to see his double sitting behind him in the crow's-nest. But of course there was nobody there. The voice had come from Squawk. He was mimicking Max and throwing his voice up to the top of the mast, so it sounded like Max was doing the talking!

"What did you say?" Becky shook her fist skyward. "Say that again and I'll have you for fish bait."

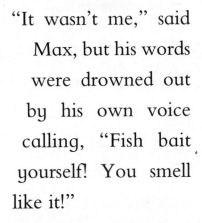

"It wasn't me," said Max, but his words were drowned out by his own voice calling, "Fish bait yourself! You smell like it!"

"Squawk, stop it!"

Max had to shut Squawk up. Frantically, he slithered down the mast. His legs snagged in the rigging and he got a splinter in his hand, but he didn't dare stop. Soon he

was low enough to jump. He landed heavily, biting his tongue. Ignoring the pain, he hurtled across the main deck and threw himself at Squawk.

Squawk had been enjoying himself so much that he didn't see Max coming for him. "Guuuuurrr, get off."

"No way," said Max, clamping Squawk's beak shut.

"Get off or I'll call the animal protection society," mumbled Squawk. "I know my rights."

"What about *my*

rights?" growled Max. "My right not to end up as fish food."

Keeping one hand firmly on Squawk's beak, Max called an apology to Becky Bones and then bundled Squawk below deck and into the galley.

"Like apologizing will help," said Squawk smugly when Max let him go. "Becky'll think you're a loony tune. Insulting her one minute, then apologizing the next. That was soooo funny! I'm a good mimic, aren't I?"

Max felt his lips twitch, but he made them stay in a frown.

Squawk rubbed his head against Max's hand.

"I didn't mean to get you into trouble. I just got carried away."

"Is that an apology?" asked Max.

"Yes," said Squawk. "Am I forgiven?"

"Only if you promise not to pull a stunt like that again," said Max sternly. Then, unable to help himself, he burst into laughter.

Squawk laughed, too, rolling onto his back and kicking his claws in the air until Max tickled his belly. Then he righted himself fast.

"You can make it up to me by teaching me how to throw my voice," Max suggested. "I could use that trick at school! But now I'm going to cut up the mango that Captain Boom left for your breakfast."

"Bring me gummi bears tomorrow or I'll pull your head off," Squawk growled in the same fierce voice he'd used earlier.

"No more tricks," said Max, slicing into the mango. "Do you hear me?"

"No more tricks, and that's a promise," agreed Squawk, saluting Max with one wing.

CHAPTER SIX
AN ACCIDENT

The first day spent pet sitting for Squawk was fun but exhausting. Max really liked the sassy parrot, but he was very lively and barely stopped talking, even to breathe! Squawk didn't play any more tricks. Instead he taught Max how to project his voice, and by the end of the day, Max was quite good at it.

"Bedtime, Squawk," said Max. His voice sounded like it came from the rusty cannon.

"You're not going to lock me up, are you?" asked Squawk, swallowing his last piece of honey-coated toast.

"I am," said Max.

"Why? I promise I'll be good. I won't go up the mast. I'll go sleep in my tree."

Squawk cocked his head and made sad eyes at Max.

"Don't!" exclaimed Max, feeling guilty. "I have to lock you up. Captain Boom's worried you might get stolen."

"Stolen!"

"Yeah!" Max chuckled. "Anyone who stole you would soon bring you back! But that's not the point. I promised Captain Boom that I'd lock you up at night."

"Like he keeps his promises," said Squawk. "His favorite saying is *That's a promise*, but he never keeps any of them."

"Oh," exclaimed Max. "So that's why he didn't fix the gangplank!"

"That's right," said Squawk. "Captain Boom keeps promising to take me for a ride on a real boat—one that doesn't leak. But he hasn't done that yet either!"

"I'm sure he will," soothed Max. "Now please get into your aviary. It's bedtime, and I've got to go home for dinner."

Squawk waddled across the deck in his ungainly style, but he stopped at the aviary door.

"Don't bother locking it," he said. "I can get out."

"How?" asked Max.

Squawk tapped his beak with a wing.

"Like I'd tell you."

"Promise me you won't do anything silly," said Max.

"Like you care!"

"I do, actually," said Max. "But I've always had a soft spot for nuts!"

"Very funny, I'm sure," said Squawk, flapping into the aviary. "Watch out, Max! I'll get you for that!"

"In your dreams," said Max, padlocking the aviary door. "And I hope they're sweet ones. Night, Squawk. See you tomorrow."

Max slept so deeply that he didn't hear his alarm ringing. The sun woke him, squeezing through a gap in the curtains. Leaping out of bed, Max pulled on his clothes.

"Squawk is not going to be happy with me," he panted as he raced for the bathroom.

Alice was in there, and no amount of

banging on the door would get her out. Max gave up on taking a shower. He waved a comb at his unruly hair, grabbed a piece of toast from the plate on the table, and bolted out to the shed to get his bike. He pedaled to the marina so fast that his tires almost smoked. He didn't slow down until he'd chained his bike to the *Leaky Dip*'s mooring and was halfway up the gangplank. Then he stopped dead. The gangplank was wobbling ominously.

"Not so fast," he told himself.

Slowly, Max took one step. The gangplank groaned. Max waited for it to settle and then took another careful step. This time the gangplank juddered and then suddenly plunged into the water, tipping Max in, too. "Urrrgh!" Max gasped in surprise.

He trod water for a moment to get his

bearings. He was halfway between the *Leaky Dip* and the shore. Max was deciding which way to swim when the gangplank floated up behind him and bopped him on the head. He spluttered and sank under the water, and when he surfaced, a long strand of seaweed was stuck to his face. Max thought he heard a giggle, but he was too busy trying to stay afloat to wonder about it. His clothes and sneakers were full of water, and the extra weight was pulling him down.

Panting like a dog, Max struck out for the *Leaky Dip*. But he hadn't realized how high the boat's deck was above the water's surface. He couldn't quite reach it, and with each failed attempt he swallowed another mouthful of salty water.

"Hang on!" called a voice.

Max heard something whizzing through the air and then felt another blow to the back of his head. It pushed him under, and when he surfaced again, coughing up more water, he found that his arms were pinned to his sides.

"Argh!" Max yelped.

He struggled fiercely until he realized he was fighting with a life preserver. Wiggling like a caterpillar, he squeezed first one arm and then the other over the top of the ring.

"Hurrah!"

From the handrail of the *Leaky Dip*, Squawk cheered wildly.

"Squawk! How did . . . ?" Max broke off, suddenly realizing that the current was pulling him toward the *Shark's Teeth*.

CHAPTER SEVEN
A TRUE PROMISE

"**E**r, morning," Max called out politely.

Becky Bones was only little, but her loud voice made up for her slight frame.

"What do you think you're doing?" she bellowed.

"Erm, I'm taking a bath," said Max, splashing water over his face. "I'm running late this morning; there was a line for the bathroom—"

"This is a marina," Becky cut in angrily, "not a hotel. I'm trying to practice my sword dance and you're distracting me. I almost chopped off my toe just then. Come any closer and I'll make you walk the plank."

"Nice to meet you, too," muttered Max, frantically kicking his skinny legs against the current as he fought his way back to the *Leaky Dip*.

"Go, Max," yelled Squawk excitedly.

The parrot moved down and began pulling at something on the deck. Suddenly a bundle of rope slithered over the side and into the water.

"Yo!" screeched Squawk as the rope ladder unfolded.

Gratefully, Max reached out and climbed aboard the *Leaky Dip*. Water gushed off him, and a shell fell out of his sneakers when he pulled them off.

Squawk hopped up and down the handrail screeching with laughter.

"That was a good one!" he shouted. "That was my best ever."

"What do you mean?" asked Max coldly. "And how did you get out of your aviary?"

"Told you I could!" Squawk stopped laughing and looked smug. "It's easy. I picked the lock. But I didn't expect you to fall in. That was wild!"

"What do you mean?"

"The gangplank joke. You weren't supposed to fall in the water. Just slip a little to give you a fright."

"You set me up? But you promised there'd be no more tricks."

"We don't keep promises on the *Leaky Dip*," said Squawk.

"Well, it's about time you did, shrimp

face!" spluttered Max. "You could have drowned me."

"Keep your feathers on," said Squawk calmly. "You sound like Becky Bones. It was a joke. No harm done."

"No harm done? Look at me!" said Max.

"So you're a bit wet! What's the big deal? You can borrow something to change into. Captain Boom has lots of clothes."

"That's okay, then," said Max sarcastically, "'cause we're about the same size, aren't we?"

Squawk's face fell. "Oooh, I didn't think of that. Never mind. You'll soon dry in the sun, and there's a good sea breeze."

Max glared at Squawk, thinking of all the horrible things he'd like to do to the parrot to get him back. Then he heard his own voice repeating: "I'm taking a bath. I'm running late this morning; there was a line for the bathroom."

Then Becky's rougher tones answered, "This is a marina, not a hotel."

Squawk was so good at mimicking Becky that Max couldn't help but laugh. And once he'd started laughing, he saw the funny side of Squawk's joke and he laughed even more. Squawk joined in. He lay on his back and, kicking his claws in the air, giggled hysterically. Max tried that, too, kicking his

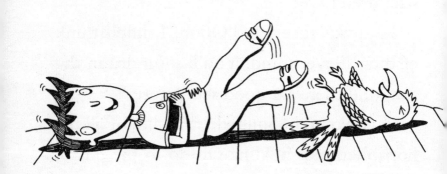

legs in the air, until, remembering his pet-sitting duties, he sat up.

"I'll go get your breakfast. I think it's oats with linseed oil and kiwifruit today."

"Yum, yum," said Squawk. "I'll just sit here in the sun and let you wait on me."

"Fine," said Max. "But no more tricks, okay?"

"I promise," said Squawk.

"A true promise, not a *Leaky Dip* one?"

"A true promise," agreed Squawk. "Don't be long. I'm starving!"

Max squelched down to the galley to prepare Squawk's breakfast. He peeled and sliced the kiwifruit and then arranged it over the oats. Next he drizzled linseed oil on top. Pleased with his efforts, Max carried the dish of food back on deck to Squawk.

"Yummy," said Squawk, swiping a piece

of kiwifruit before Max had even put the dish down.

"Slow down." Max laughed. "You'll make yourself sick."

While Squawk gobbled his breakfast, Max cleaned up the aviary. Then he went down to the galley to refill Squawk's bowl of water.

As Max stepped back on deck, the *Leaky Dip* rolled suddenly. Max wobbled, almost spilling the water. Carefully, he made his way back to the aviary. The wind was getting stronger, and Max's wet clothes flapped uncomfortably. Someone was shouting. It sounded like Becky Bones. Max grinned, glad he wasn't getting told off this time. The shouting grew louder. Then there was a tremendous BANG! The *Leaky Dip* shuddered so violently that Max fell headfirst into the aviary and dropped the water bowl on his toe.

"Ouch!" he yelled, shaking his wet foot. "Squawk, what are you doing now?"

It sounded like the parrot was messing around with the old cannon. Max legged it back to the main deck, but Squawk was nowhere near the cannon. He was staring at the *Shark's Teeth*. Onboard, Captain Becky Bones was leaping in the air.

"Come back here," howled Becky, waving her sword at Max.

"Yeah, right," whispered Max. "So you can cut us up and feed us to the fish? I don't think so. What's she angry about this time?"

"Can't you guess?" Squawk's tiny eyes were bright with fear, and Max realized he was missing something.

"Guess what?"

"We just crashed into the *Shark's Teeth* and put a dent in the side."

"What? How could we?"

"Because no one's steering the boat," said Squawk.

"What are you talking about? You don't

steer a boat that's tied up in a marina."

"But we're not," whispered Squawk.
"We've come adrift. We're heading out
to sea."

CHAPTER EIGHT
SQUAWK AT SEA

Squawk hung his head.

"It was an accident," he mumbled. "I think I untied the wrong rope when I was setting up the gangplank trick."

"Great," said Max. "I feel much better now that I know you didn't mean to do it."

"Really?"

"No," said Max. "Remind me—where is the ship's wheel?"

"Over there," said Squawk, pointing a multicolored wing at a large wooden wheel on the main deck. "But . . ."

As Max ran to the ship's wheel, he tried

to remember how to steer a boat. He'd done it once before, on vacation. It wasn't like steering a bicycle or a car. You had to turn the wheel and wait for the wind to take you where you wanted to go. The *Leaky Dip*'s wheel was as battered as the rest of the ship. Carefully, Max grasped it between his skinny hands and turned it to the left. Nothing happened. Perhaps it took even longer to turn this type of boat?

Max hung on, willing the boat to turn. When it didn't, he spun the wheel around farther.

"It doesn't work very well," said

Squawk, flying over. "It's broken. Captain Boom's never bothered to fix it because the *Leaky Dip* has too many holes to go sailing in her."

"Do you have *any* good news?" snapped Max.

"Er, I don't expect we'll get that far. Not without a sail."

"We've drifted quite a way already," said Max, looking back at the marina. "The current's pulling us. We're going to have to put the sail up or we'll never get back. We'll just drift farther out."

Squawk brightened. "Does that mean I get to go up the mast?"

Max did some quick thinking. He couldn't be in two places at once, and it would probably be safer to let Squawk put the sail up than let him steer the boat.

The wheel was heavy, and Max doubted Squawk would be able to turn it.

"Okay, but no tricks. You put the sail up and come right back. This is serious, Squawk. We could drown if you mess around."

Squawk looked offended.

"I'm not an airhead," he said gruffly.

"No, you're a birdbrain," Max said, chuckling. "Now go get that sail up. We're almost out on the open sea."

Enthusiastically, Squawk flew off to unfurl the mainsail. Max, a hand shielding his green eyes from the sun, watched as the bird untied each of the ropes that bound the sail to the mast. But his relief was short-lived. As the sail began to unfold, Max saw that it was full of holes. When Squawk finally returned to the deck, Max couldn't help commenting, "It's got more holes than your granny's underpants."

Squawk groaned and then tucked his head under his wing.

"It wasn't that funny," said Max.

"Not laughing," moaned Squawk. "I don't feel well. I feel sick."

"You probably ate your breakfast too fast," said Max unsympathetically. "I always eat that fast," said Squawk.

"This is different. I feel awful. Stop the boat from going up and down!"

"So sorry—I'll try to find a flat part of the sea!"

Max wiggled the ship's wheel.

"No, can't find any flat parts. It's got something to do with these pesky waves!" he said with even more sarcasm.

"I'm going to be . . ."

Then Squawk lurched forward and threw up all over Max's shoe.

Gross! thought Max. Then, remembering that he was the pet sitter, he pulled a very damp tissue from his pocket and carefully wiped Squawk's beak.

"Better now?"

"Noooooo," moaned Squawk. "Not better. I want to go back. Don't like it out here. The sea's too wobbly."

"You get seasick?" Max was incredulous. "Whoever heard of a pirate's parrot suffering from seasickness?"

"Runs in the family," Squawk whimpered. "My uncle ran away with a circus 'cause the sea makes him so sick."

"Do you want to go sit in your tree? I'll carry you there if you like."

"Noooo," groaned Squawk. "I want to lie down."

"Should I make you a bed?"

"Yes, please."

Max looked at the junk around him. There was plenty there to make Squawk a comfortable bed. With one hand still on the ship's wheel, Max stretched out and managed to pull a battered old crate toward him. Then, hooking a piece of sailcloth over his foot, he lifted that over, too. The sailcloth fitted perfectly inside the crate. Max quickly let go of the ship's wheel to help Squawk get into his new bed.

"Is that better?"

"Yes," said Squawk, "but I wouldn't mind a drink of water."

Max looked around. They'd safely passed all the boats in the marina and had almost reached the open sea. Max knew a little about wind and how it affected the direction a boat could take. Once out at sea, Max hoped to sail the *Leaky Dip* in a circle to bring her back to the marina. At the speed they were traveling, he probably had enough time to run down to the galley and get Squawk some water before he made the turn.

"I'll be one second," he said.

Faster than a galleon in a gale, Max raced to the galley. He filled a bowl with water and then rushed back to find that Squawk had fallen asleep.

"Great," said Max. He was thirsty himself now, but he didn't dare leave the ship's wheel again. The *Leaky Dip* was already drifting away to the left. Max fixed his eye on a red buoy and steered toward it. At first the boat didn't seem to respond, but after awhile Max was happy they were traveling in the direction he wanted to go. Enviously, he watched a sleek boat coming up fast behind the *Leaky Dip*. The boat had three masts, each with a pennant flying from the top. Max squinted at the pennants, trying to figure out what was on them. A sudden boom made him jump. Something whistled through the air and splashed into the water a short way from the *Leaky Dip*.

"Snapping sharks!" exclaimed Max.

Now that the boat was closer, he could clearly see its three pennants. Each had a skull and crossbones, with red blood oozing from the eye sockets.

There was another bang, and Max ducked

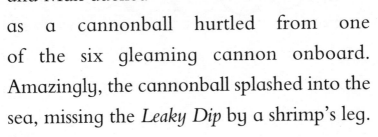

as a cannonball hurtled from one of the six gleaming cannon onboard. Amazingly, the cannonball splashed into the sea, missing the *Leaky Dip* by a shrimp's leg.

"Oh no!" groaned Max, a cold feeling stealing over him. "It's the *Shark's Teeth*, and I don't think Becky Bones is trying to invite me to lunch."

CHAPTER NINE
THE BATTLE

The noise woke Squawk. Woozily, he sat up and vomited all over Max's other shoe.

"Nice." Max sighed. "A matching pair!"

"Water," quavered Squawk. "I need a drink."

Max quickly let go of the ship's wheel to push Squawk's water bowl closer. The parrot took a few sips and then leaned against Max's leg.

"How are you feeling now?" he asked.

"As sick as a parrot," moaned Squawk.

Max stroked the parrot's head. He didn't like seeing him in this state. He preferred

Squawk the joker.

"We'll soon be home," he said, glancing back sneakily at the *Shark's Teeth*.

The rival boat was approaching fast. Max could see Captain Becky Bones furiously waving her sword at the *Leaky Dip*. She shouted something that Max couldn't hear. Max willed the *Leaky Dip* on, but if anything, she seemed to be slowing down. Max knew his only chance was to get back to the marina. It would be busy there by then. Too busy for Captain Bones to carry out her worst threats. But out there on the open sea, Max could be made to walk the plank, and only the fish would know! Were there sharks this close to the shore? Max shivered. He didn't know, and he didn't want to find out!

"Squawk," said Max casually, "where does Captain Boom keep his cannonballs?"

"Under his bunk," said Squawk. "Why?"

"Erm," Max hesitated, not sure how much to tell Squawk when he was so sick.

"Becky Bones is after us, isn't she?"

Max laughed. Squawk was too smart for his own good!

"Yes."

"That's good," said Squawk, closing his eyes. "She'll soon put me out of my misery!"

"That's not going to happen," said Max. "We'll be back in the marina soon, and then you'll feel better."

He glanced at the *Shark's Teeth* again. The boat was definitely gaining on the *Leaky Dip*. Max didn't have any choice. He would have to leave the wheel in order to fetch a supply of cannonballs. Gently, he lifted Squawk back into his makeshift bed.

"Stay there," he said.

"Like I'm going anywhere else," muttered the parrot.

Once again, Max raced below deck. Captain Boom's cabin was easily the messiest place onboard the ship. Max waded through dirty clothes, towels, and a mountain of *Pirate Weekly* magazines until he reached the bunk. He scrabbled around underneath it, pulling out more junk until he found what he was looking for—a rusty iron ball a bit smaller than a soccer ball.

"Is that it?" muttered Max, feeling under the bunk again. "There must be more than one."

But there wasn't. Disappointed, Max

carried the cannonball back on deck. The *Shark's Teeth* was much closer now. The moment Max took hold of the *Leaky Dip*'s wheel, Becky Bones started shouting at him again. Max closed his ears and concentrated on steering the boat back toward the harbor.

They were making very slow progress. The *Leaky Dip* groaned and leaned sharply to the right. Max hung on to the wheel and used his foot to stop Squawk's bed from sliding away. Then Max noticed the water. The deck was like a wading pool. Max, whose sneakers were still wet after his early-morning swim, was shocked that he hadn't noticed the flooded deck before.

"Snapping sharks!" he exclaimed. "We're sinking."

"Man the lifeboat," said Squawk weakly.

Max brightened.

"Good idea. Where is it?"

"There isn't one. Captain Boom keeps promising to buy one, but . . ." Squawk shrugged his wings.

"Another *Leaky Dip* promise," Max said with a sigh.

As fast as the *Leaky Dip* was filling up with water, the *Shark's Teeth* was getting closer. Max gave up trying to steer while he prepared the cannon.

"We're going down fighting," he said.

"Matches in the locker over there," said Squawk.

Luckily, the water hadn't reached the locker. Pocketing the matches, Max loaded the cannonball and took aim. The *Shark's Teeth* drew alongside the *Leaky Dip*. Max heard scrabbling, like an enormous rat, and then Captain Becky Bones climbed up over the handrail, a rope in her mouth.

"Hold your fire," she said with her mouth full.

"Yeah, right!" muttered Max, lighting the match.

There was a muffled bang, followed by a small thud. A thick cloud of black dust burst from the end of the cannon. Then the cannonball plopped out and rolled across the *Leaky Dip*'s wet deck. Max coughed and wiped the dust from his eyes. Typical! Even the cannon didn't work properly.

"I should have guessed," groaned Max, wishing he'd thought to arm himself. Even a frying pan would have been better than nothing. But it was too late now.

"Shiver me shoes!" roared Captain Becky

Bones, leaping aboard. "What part of *hold your fire* didn't you understand?"

Deftly, she tied the *Shark's Teeth*'s mooring rope to a ring on deck, and then, spitting on her hand, she rubbed at her sooty face.

"I don't know why I'm bothering to rescue you," she said fiercely.

Max stared in amazement. He was so scared that his brain was having trouble figuring everything out.

"Rescue us? But you've just tried to sink us with cannonballs."

"That was to get your attention. I'd have hit you if I'd wanted to."

"You've really come to save us?"

"Yes," growled Becky Bones, as if she hadn't really wanted to. "Your boat's dangerous. It's too full of holes to sail anywhere."

"But why would you help us?"

"I owe Captain Boom a favor. When I accidentally cut off my finger practicing sword moves, Captain Boom drove me to the hospital, where a nice doctor sewed it back on. See?" Proudly, Becky Bones showed Max a slanted finger with a neat scar at its base.

"Captain Boom always seems a little scared of me, but I couldn't let the *Leaky Dip* sink. I might not get such a helpful neighbor next time."

Max grinned with relief. "That's lucky."

"It will be if we make it back. You're not out of the water yet!" Becky Bones laughed at her own joke. "Better get a move on before I change my mind and leave you to sink!"

CHAPTER TEN
ONE MORE PROMISE

The trip back to the marina was long and slow. Even being towed, Max still had to steer the *Leaky Dip* while baling out the water at the same time. He also had to take care of Squawk. But once they were safely back in their old mooring, the sick parrot perked up quickly, until Becky produced a list of chores that she wanted done in order to make up for the dent in the *Shark's Teeth*.

"As sick as a parrot," wailed Squawk when Max told him that their first job was to scrub the decks.

"You'll be sicker than a parrot if you

don't lend a wing," said Max sternly. "I'll lock you in your aviary, and this time I'll use the padlock from my bicycle chain. It's a number combination, so you won't be able to pick that!"

"Huh! You're meaner than Becky's bones!" joked Squawk.

"What's that about my bones?"

Squawk jumped guiltily, but there was no one there.

"What . . . ?"

Max grinned.

"Get a move on, birdbrain," he said in Becky's gruff voice.

Squawk laughed.

"Nice one, Max. You had me fooled."

"Good," said Max. "But no more jokes. It's time to work."

* * *

Squawk and Max
sat on a branch in
Squawk's tree, watching
for Captain Boom, who
was due home any
minute.

"There he is!" shouted
Squawk excitedly as a
battered car pulled up
next to the *Leaky
Dip*'s gangplank. "Last
one down's a dodo."

Squawk launched himself

from the branch and flew toward the gangplank. Max slithered down the tree trunk. He was miles behind Squawk but still in time to see Captain Boom stumble on the wobbly gangplank and almost fall into the water.

"I'll fix that today, and that's a promise," puffed Captain Boom as he stepped on deck. "Hello, you two. How did it go?"

"Good, thanks," said Max. "How was Treasure?"

"Same as usual. How was Squawk?"

"He was good."

"Really?" Captain Boom sounded surprised. "What—no tricks, no jokes? He didn't upset Captain Becky Bones even once?"

"Erm, Squawk was Squawk," said Max truthfully.

Captain Boom stared at Squawk, and Squawk stared innocently back.

"So you'd look after him again?"

"Yes, I'd definitely pet sit for you again." Max winked at Squawk. "And that's a promise!"

Me and Squawk!

ABOUT THE AUTHOR

Julie Sykes has had more than thirty books
published, including several about her
creation Little Tiger. Among her other titles
are *That Pesky Dragon, Dora's Eggs,* and
Hurry, Santa! Her books *I Don't Want
to Go to Bed!* and *I Don't Want to
Have a Bath!* won the Nottingham
Children's Book Award. Julie has three
children and lives in Hampshire, England.

ABOUT THE ILLUSTRATOR

Nathan Reed has illustrated children's
stories for Puffin, HarperCollins, and
Campbell Books. He also illustrated one
of the most popular titles in Kingfisher's
I Am Reading series, *Hocus Pocus Hound.*
Nathan lives in London, England.

INHALT